P9-CCQ-406

Originally published in German in 1909 as *Prinzeßchen im Walde*
English version by Polly Lawson © Floris Books, Edinburgh 1994
British Library CIP data available
ISBN 0-86315-189-2
Printed in Belgium

The Princess
in the Forest

Sibylle von Olfers

Floris Books

In the heart of the forest, there the princess lives in her castle. Every morning, she wakes and looks out of her window. She sees the dew maids coming through the trees.

By the stream, the dew maids help the princess to wash and dress. They brush her hair. They put on her golden shoes. They put on her royal cloak.

The princess sits under the trees. The moss boys bring her breakfast. The princess likes honey and jelly and fruits of the forest.

Now the princess has her lessons. She writes on a black slate with a golden border. Mrs Crow is her teacher. Mrs Crow is very wise.

Lessons are over! It's time to play with friends. Come along, little deer! Come along, hares and squirrels and birds!

At the edge of the forest, there live the mushroom children and the toadstool children. The princess likes to tell them stories.

The day is ending. Now the princess must go home. The star folk come to light her way through the trees.

It is night time. The folk of the forest are all asleep. In the castle, the princess is asleep as well. But one little star keeps watch all night.